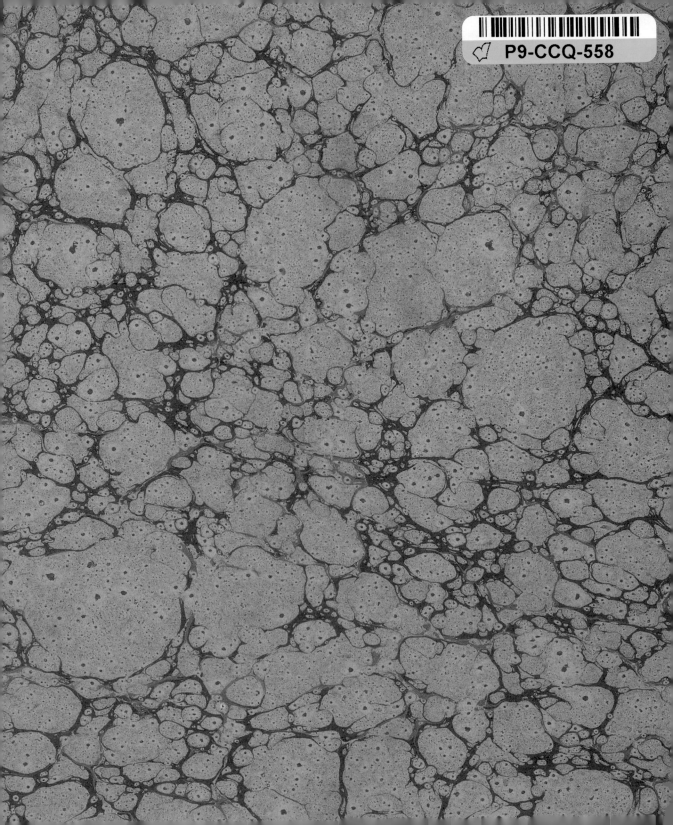

From the last will and testament of Rafael Hurtago:

To my grandson, Armon Hurt, I leave my house in

Ronda, Spain, and the uncertainty of its contents.

May he discover his belonging.

THE
FORGET

Nick Bantock

TING ROOM

a fiction

A BYZANTIUM BOOK

HarperCollins*Publishers*

TO MY FAMILY

Acknowledgments: Ruth Kasasian and Alexandra Goodall, for
their young Armon drawings; Dawna Stromsoe, for bringing *duende*
to my attention; Katherine Wilding, for her suggestions; Erika Berg,
for her work in the book's early stages.
Page 5: Karl Baedeker. *Espagne et Portugal: Manuel du voyageur,*
2ème éd. Leipzig: Karl Baedeker, 1908.

Every attempt has been made to trace accurate ownership of
copyrighted visual material in this book. Errors and omissions
will be corrected in subsequent editions, provided notification
is sent to the publisher.

The author wishes to point out that any misquotes or mistranslations of
García Lorca's writings are attributable to the book's fictional characters.

Art direction: Barbara Hodgson / Byzantium Books Inc.
Book and jacket design: Isabelle Swiderski / Byzantium Books Inc.
Composition: Byzantium Books Inc.
Jacket art: Nick Bantock
Jacket photographer: Robert Keziere
Text photography: Smith Photo Prints

THE FORGETTING ROOM

HarperCollins books may be purchased for educational, business, or sales
promotional use. For information please write: Special Markets Department,
HarperCollins Publishers, Inc., 10 East 53rd Street, New York, NY 10022.

FIRST EDITION
Library of Congress Cataloging-in-Publication Data:
  Bantock, Nick.
        The forgetting room : a novel / Nick Bantock.
           p.   cm.
        ISBN 0-00-225176-0
        I. Title
     PR6052.A54F67 1997
        823' .914—dc21   96-51665
97 98 99 00 01 ❖/HK 10 9 8 7 6 5 4 3 2

Shortly after my return to Massachusetts, I found myself wishing I'd kept a diary during the nine days I was in Ronda. Before my memories could fade, I set about confirming the solidity of the arc, and recording the events.

Later when my account grew pictures, I decided to bind the words and images together in book form.

The following is a limited edition of one.

ESPAGNE
OCCIDENTALE
ET
PORTUGAL

ARMON—7

Armon II

❧ Until I was eleven years old I spent my vacations with my grandfather Rafael and grandmother Marianne in their house in a small village thirty miles east of my home city of Geneva. Almost every day I'd sit in Grandfather's studio watching him paint and listening to him talk about whatever came into his mind. Mostly his words were too grown-up for me and sailed blithely over my head, but his deep, gentle voice was as reassuring as the warm cocoa Grandmother plied us with on winter afternoons. At the end of each day Grandfather would clean his brushes, stand, shake himself like a large dog, and proceed with my ritual drawing lesson. I basked in his full attention, and the rudiments of draftsmanship came easily to me, though it was hard to tell whether this was brought about by his good teaching or my enthusiasm.

In 1972 my father's factory, la Compagnie impériale des boîtes de carton (The Box), was amalgamated with a U.S. firm, and Father agreed to supervise a new plant in Chicago.

In the same week that he signed the contract that committed our family to life on a different continent, a forest fire engulfed my grandparents' house and burned it to the ground. Instead of rebuilding, my grandparents decided to keep the insurance money and move to my grandfather's family home in Ronda. For a reason not clear to me, and despite my family's imminent departure to America, I felt deserted by my grandparents' retreat to Spain.

Although he wrote to me regularly, and I occasionally responded with a short letter or postcard, my grandfather and I never saw each other again. The close company we once kept seemed to act as a barrier that I was unable to overcome. The memory of my innocent acceptance of his caring was a threat to the self-contained person I became.

For his part, Grandfather twice planned to visit us in the States, but on both occasions Grandmother's failing health prevented their trip.

Three months ago my grandfather died, leaving me his house. I was confused by his death—I wasn't ready for him to die and felt quite unworthy of inheriting his property.

Financially it was the windfall my bookbinding workshop needed, but the idea of selling my grandfather's house troubled me deeply. I decided to fly to Spain to see the property before I put it on the market.

⊰ DAY ONE ⊱

🐦 **The bus ride from Málaga** took me through Torre-molinos, Marbella, along the northern coastline of the Mediterranean, and it made me irritable. When Rafael was a boy there must have been an almost uninterrupted view of the sea from the road, but now it was blocked out by a seemingly endless parade of candy-pink condos and pasteboard hotels. I've always hated that kind of inane uglification. And to see it perpetrated in my grandfather's homeland made it all the worse.

The climb into the mountains lifted my spirits, though the winding roads left me sleepy and I must have nodded off. I surfaced again on the approach to Ronda. Through the window I took in the great wedge-shaped hill and saw my romantic expectations both confirmed and damned. To the left, perched high on the edge of an almost vertical escarpment, were the baked amber and white walls of an ancient fortress town, but to the right, leading away from the old stones, a small urban sprawl trailed its way down the long, steady slope of the hill's spine.

When I got off the bus I discovered the terminal wasn't on

my antiquated map and I couldn't work out where I was. I had a moment's panic, but it passed and after randomly threading my way through the narrow streets I bumbled into the elegant confines of the Plaza del Socorro.

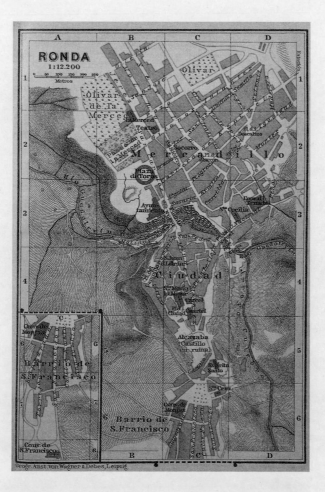

I sat at the café on the corner of the square, with my bag secure between my legs, and let out a long breath. I liked the place. The square was friendly, large enough to accommodate a herd of noisy kids playing soccer, but not so big (like its Italian counterparts) that it would cause agoraphobia.

I had an hour to kill before my five o'clock appointment when I would pick up the keys to my grandfather's house. Once I'd ordered a drink I permitted my mind to return (for the millionth time) to my chief preoccupation—the frustrations of running an archaic one-man business on a shoestring. Disposing of Grandfather's house in order to subsidize the workshop seemed my only course of action, but it felt disrespectful, and I was trying to ignore my discomfort over the inheritance by being ultrapractical about a quick sale. If I'd still been married to Catherine, I'm sure she would have tried to get me to articulate my ambivalence. She would also have argued that the influx of money be used to cut back the number of hours I worked. I liked the amount of time I spent in the workshop; it gave me a sense of purpose.

Even in its imaginary form, it was a very old argument, and as usual we were speaking different languages. My internal conversation with Catherine fell silent, as our real ones often had.

On the plane I'd been picking fitfully at a volume of quotes, seeking out suitable lines to incorporate within Ex Libris labels. When I opened the book again I found myself confronting the dry words of E. Arnold—

Never shalt thou build again these walls of pain . . .
Ye suffer from yourself . . . and whirl upon the wheel,
and hug and kiss its spokes of agony.

Under the circumstances it was depressingly close to home. I put the book down and watched the soccer-mad children weaving in and out of the people crossing the square—the tourists cutting the corners, the locals plowing through the heart of the makeshift playing field. Time passed. I glanced down and saw that somebody had left a scuffed matchbox on the table. The picture on the front mimicked the scene in the square. I like that kind of coinci-dence—it gave me the reassuring notion that there was a grand order to things. It was sort of liberating. I had the embarrassing urge to rush out into the melee and hog the ball. I saw myself dribbling round the opposing team and driving the ball into the back of the net (between the two rolled-up coats that were acting as goalposts) and raising my fist to the heavens in salute.

I was summoned from my daydreams by a distant clock reminding me that I needed to get going. I paid for my drink and made for the old town. It only took me a couple of minutes to get to the bridge, which divides the new town from the old. This "new bridge," which is higher up and not new at all, just newer than the old bridge, spans a fearsome three-hundred-feet-wide gorge. No amount of guidebook reading prepares you for the awe that strikes the first time you cross the Puente Nuevo, look over the edge, and see the sheer five hundred feet of water-gouged chasm dropping away to a minute stony riverbed far below. It breeds pure vertigo.

To my relief Ciudad (the old town) really was exactly as I'd hoped it might be. There were hardly any tourists for a start, and although the buildings were partly restored, they carried their age with a lofty dignity.

I checked my watch, to make certain I wasn't late, and was intrigued by the way my olive skin seemed to blend with the ocher and rust of the buildings' facades. I was so used to being Swiss-American, it was always a surprise when my Spanish blood crept up on me.

I was due to collect the keys from Francesca and Paolo Ete, my grandfather's oldest friends, who lived not far from the Mondragon Palace ("Palace" being a misleadingly expansive name for what I later found to be a largish house—albeit fascinating and quite beautiful).

I arrived at the Etes' tiled porch just after five and was courteously greeted by a slim woman, of around seventy, with short gray hair and equally gray eyes. Señora Ete invited me in and said if I cared to rest my feet and wait for her husband, who would be returning soon, they would walk me to Rafael's house. I thanked her but said if she'd give me directions I'd find my own way. She told me she quite understood that I must be tired and handed me the keys with a sympathetic smile, telling me that she'd been to the house regularly, watering the plants and making certain that I would see it as my grandfather would have wished. Her kindness (as all kindnesses from strangers) unnerved me and I was unsure how to respond. As I was leaving she insisted that I return the following evening for dinner. She said her husband had something for me. Something my grandfather had given him to pass on to me.

Calle Ruedo Don Elvina wasn't as difficult to find as I expected. It's a small street, but being next to the House of the Moorish Kings, it's hard to miss.

Rafael's house was on the corner of a shallow alley. It was a handsome two-and-a-half-storied building that appeared to be in good condition apart from the crumbling stucco just below the roofline. The west-facing white wall was ceremoniously draped in a saffron glow from the evening sun. The upper windows were shuttered and the three-grilled lower windows (two at the front, one at the side) displayed rows of well-kempt geraniums. The overall effect of the place was of the soft, unfussy care and attention I associated with my grandmother. I concluded that Rafael had kept it to her taste, even when he had been left behind to look after it on his own.

The house had one truly distinctive feature—a hefty, arch-topped front door, with a star and a row of three crescent moons carved into its face.

The key turned in the lock without a struggle, and in joint awe and feigned indifference I stepped into my grandfather's domain.

In terms of size Rafael's home was much as I'd expected. Downstairs consisted of a living room/dining room and kitchen. The kitchen was small and neat. The living room was large and airy. The second floor held a bedroom and a bathroom. The attic—though I could only guess at this because the door was locked—I took to be a studio. The rooms had obviously been kept spotless by Señora Ete and the house felt lived in. One thing did strike me as curious though: there were none of Rafael's pictures on the walls. After a moment's consideration, I decided they were probably all in the studio.

I kept wandering around the house, not quite sure what to do. On my third circuit I peeped behind the hall curtain and found a cellar door that I'd missed on the first two rounds, but that, too, was locked. I felt tired and jet-lagged, my stomach was making grumbly noises, and I had no desire to go key searching.

In the bedroom I became preoccupied trying to work out which of the twin beds was my grandfather's and which one I wanted to sleep in. Eventually I pushed them together to make a double. The effort totally exhausted me.

I collapsed onto the bed. Realizing I'd fall asleep in my clothes if I didn't undress there and then, I stood up and stripped. I could hear noises from outside; I half wondered what they were, but my curiosity was no match for the lure of the pillow.

✢ DAY TWO ✢

✺ **I awoke around six** with a sense of urgency—I wanted to examine my inheritance and to look for Grandfather's pictures, so I started a more detailed exploration of the house. For reasons of restraint or reverence I tried to do it in silence, but the place utterly refused to cooperate. Everything I touched had an almost comical vocal response. Even the stairs refused to let me descend in peace—each step creaking its idiosyncratic tone.

In the kitchen cupboard I found two keys. The first unlocked the cellar, which contained little more than an ocean of cobwebs. The second, as I expected, unlocked the studio.

As soon as I stepped into the room the smell hit me—a conglomeration of linseed, turpentine, and everything else that was the essence of my grandfather. It looked just like his studio in Switzerland. The layout was of course different, but the mixture of comfortable-looking old furniture, strangely contrived artifacts, and stacked art material was exactly the same.

It is odd, but I don't think I understood he was dead until that point. It was being in his studio without him, with all his equipment laid out ready for work and no one to use it. I started to choke up but wouldn't let myself. I marched straight over to the window, stared very hard at the light on the distant hills, then turned back to face the room. I took it in, in more detail, walked back to the door, turned again, and faced the room as if entering for the first time.

The windows were surrounded by floor-to-ceiling wooden shelving. The lower shelves were crammed full of paints, brushes, jars of charcoal, bottles of varnish, pots of glue, and everything else he needed for his profession. The upper shelves housed a collection of objects, some of which looked like they belonged in a museum and others, like the half section of a clarinet surmounted by a moon globe, had clearly been adapted to suit Rafael's surreal tastes.

Piled against the right-hand wall were dismantled stretcher frames, drawing boards, and old bits of wood, along with boxes of assorted "stuff."

A workbench was pressed against the left-hand wall, along with a tall, glass-fronted cabinet containing similar but smaller items of dubious origin. Behind me was a cupboard that opened to reveal yet more things, and more boxes filled with old newspapers and magazines.

The bare floorboards by the side of the workbench were stained and paint splattered and gave away Rafael's preference for working close to the ground, on his hands and knees.

The other end of the room was less busy, with a small beaten-up Persian rug, an invitingly worn horsehair sofa, and a small, low mahogany table.

Yet there were still no paintings, no drawings, nothing. Surely they hadn't been stolen. It occurred to me that it might have been one of Rafael's games—did he want me to find the pictures? Could that have been what the will had meant by ". . . discover his belonging"? As a child I would probably have been bubbling over with curiosity, but as a confirmed adult all I could feel was irritation that Rafael was making things difficult.

I'd already started for the door when I saw the red pigskin bundle, tied with a black thong, that Rafael used to keep all his favorite tools in. I picked it up, remembering fondly its weight and leathery softness. I didn't want to let go of it, so I took it downstairs and reverently unwrapped it on the kitchen table. The pouch contained my grandfather's best pencils, pens, scissors, and brushes. They seemed so precious, almost magical, and I struggled with the demands they made on me. When I was nine or ten, Rafael had said to me that one day they would be mine, but now they made me nervous. It felt like too much responsibility. He had believed I shared his creative fire, but I felt none of the flame. I didn't want his expectations, and I rewrapped the bundle, quickly slipping it into the table drawer.

I grabbed my jacket and went out to pick up some coffee, fruit, bread, and juice for breakfast. While I was taking my wallet out of my inside pocket to pay for the groceries, I inadvertently pulled out a photograph that I'd shoved into the pocket a few weeks before. Grandmother had sent the photo to me years ago, when she and Rafael moved to Spain. It was just a snapshot of a local scene, but until my arrival it represented my vision of Ronda and I'd carried it with me while I was deciding whether to make the trip.

Back in the kitchen, chewing on dry bread (I'd forgotten the butter), I looked at the photo again. It was tempting and I ruminated on slipping out to look over the town, but then I convinced myself that it was more appropriate to do what I'd come here for, to go through the house and make notes about what to keep and what to get rid of. I was giving myself a hard time, being a martyr to self-imposed obligation as well as feeling callous for planning to dispose of things that I didn't feel I really owned.

I began with the living room and the kitchen, thinking I'd work my way from bottom to top.

Before I started, I took out the leather bundle from the drawer and went back to the studio to return it. The room fascinated me. I wanted to stay and look at all its contents. But I resisted.

By late morning I'd semi-finished downstairs. The kitchen was straightforward; I'd give away or sell the contents apart from a couple of nice old knives I took a fancy to. The living room, on the other hand, was harder to sort through. I started to get bogged down, choosing between what I liked and what I wanted. I pretended to make decisions though I couldn't work out the criteria by which to judge.

I moved up to my grandfather's bedroom and began on his personal effects. Apart from the twin beds, there were a tall chest of drawers made out of an unusually grained wood, like cherry or maybe pear; a straight-backed chair; an almost empty wardrobe, probably once used by my grandmother Marianne; and a bookcase jammed tight with books. The walls were gray-blue and the floorboards were stained alternately blue and black. It felt cool and dreamy in there and by noon I'd done nothing. I'd picked things up, put them down, opened drawers, and closed them again without disturbing the contents. I thought about lunch, decided I wasn't that hungry, and tried again. I really wanted to examine the studio in more detail, but I stuck to the task I'd set for myself. I was wriggling on a hook. I didn't want to have to touch another person's everyday things. The hairbrush in the bathroom still held a few strands of his hair.

In the end it was an old sweater with a distinctive pattern and a discolored shoulder that did it. He'd been wearing it the last time I saw him twenty-three years ago, and when I found it in the bottom of a drawer, the loss I'd been hiding from caught up with me.

After the tears it was much easier to carry on.

As I put the sweater back I thought about the way I'd let all those years pass without even coming to visit him. Catherine was right; I sure could procrastinate when it came to the big things.

Around six I finally called it a day. I was due at the Etes' house at seven and I wanted to get myself cleaned up before I went.

Paolo turned out to be a giant, six four or five, and around two hundred and twenty pounds. His hair was white and wavy, and he looked like he would live to be a hundred. When he saw me, he grinned from ear to ear and ushered me into the house. He had a face devoid of anxiety and looked as if he'd gone without a moment's worry all his life. I liked him in spite of my envy. He sat me down in the best chair, and we talked while Francesca cooked and occasionally interjected enthusiastically from the kitchen. We spoke of

Ronda and its geological uniqueness. He said he'd hardly been away from the town since he was born, apart from when he traveled to Switzerland for Rafael's wedding. I said I realized he'd known Rafael for some while, but I had no idea it was that long. He laughed and said, "Longer than that; we were at school together. I was a year younger than Rafael. You wouldn't believe it to look at me now, but as a boy I was skinny and weak. Rafael befriended me and kept the bullies from picking on me. I loved him like a brother. I truly miss him."

Dinner turned out to be a mountainous paella, piled on a huge silver plate that Paolo trumpeted in, in mock ceremony. While we were eating, I asked about Rafael and Marianne's wedding. Paolo described it with hand-waving exuberance, making it sound like a cross between a Bacchanalian feast and a Dadaist dream.

"I wish I could have been there," I said.

To which he responded, "You know, I'm certain I've still got the wedding invitation somewhere." He went to a desk in a corner of the room and after a second or two of searching came back and handed me the card.

When I reached out to take it from him, I felt a strange wave of anticipation. It must have shown because Francesca said to Paolo, "Why don't you let him keep it? It's of no use to you now."

With gentle formality and only the slightest hesitation, Paolo said, "Certainly. For Rafael's grandson, I could do no less."

LE
Ma
ria
de
ge

2 7 o.c.tto.b.r.e.1.9.4.0

I tried to refuse, but they both insisted. I told them I would treasure it—which was absolutely true.

I asked if they knew how Rafael and Marianne had met. Paolo said Rafael never gave him the same version of the story twice. Then gesturing to his wife he said, "But Marianne confided in Francesca."

Francesca said that was true and she knew all about Marianne and Rafael's first encounter:

It was just before the Second World War and Marianne was twenty-five years old, living in Paris, and as unattached as anyone could be. One night, in the Café Tzara, she had just finished reading a set of her poems to an audience that divided its interest equally between her words and her legs, when an earnest young man had come up to her and told her he thought the poems "Magnificent." The verse he particularly enthused over was about the taunting of death. Marianne took in his black hair and dark eyes and without difficulty guessed him to be Spanish. She was finding his childlike intensity too demanding and was beginning to turn away when he put his hand on her arm. She felt a warmth run through her. He smiled and changed from a boy to a grown man. He said, "I'm not quite as serious as you think. Will you sit and talk with me for a while?"

Marianne didn't fall in love at first sight, but neither did it take her all evening to lose her heart.

When the war broke out in 1939, they moved, like many

painters, musicians, and writers, to the safety of Switzerland. They married in Geneva and stayed on in the city after the Allied victory in France. The rest you probably know about. They were very close. It was hard on Rafael when Marianne died.

The mention of Marianne's death jabbed awake my sleeping guilt. She had died seven years ago. When I found out, I'd checked with my father to see if he was going to fly over for the funeral, but he'd said he couldn't get away. I had tried phoning my grandfather but after a few failed attempts to get through I'd given up. The truth was, I hadn't known what to say to him.

Francesca and Paolo were very easy to be with and the tales and anecdotes that poured from them enabled me to overcome my natural reserve. Neither were artists, but they loved art. They talked about Marianne's poetry and Rafael's painting. I mentioned that I couldn't find any of my grandfather's pictures in the house. They looked at each other and then Paolo said, "I thought you knew, Rafael gave all his artwork away. He sent one to each of his friends and to everyone who'd ever done him a kindness; he spread them around. He even gave a picture to the store owner whose small dog he regularly stopped to pat."

I asked if Rafael had given them one of his pictures.

"Yes," Paolo replied. "Would you like to see it? It's upstairs."

I said I would and followed him to the upper hallway. The

picture wasn't quite what I'd expected. Surprisingly abstract and restrained for Rafael, it consisted of a lonely-looking pinky-red shape sitting in isolation on a snowy-white ground. It immediately made me think of Rafael's pigskin pouch lying unused in his studio.

I didn't show it to Paolo, but I was extremely jealous. I wanted the painting for myself. Why hadn't Rafael given any pictures to me? I knew he must have had a good reason, but I was too upset to see what would later become obvious.

I stayed a little longer for politeness' sake, then around ten-thirty I arose and said, "I'd better go." I thanked them profusely for their hospitality and bid them good night. As I was leaving, Paolo said, "I have something for you, from your grandfather." He went back into the living room and returned with a flat cardboard case about nine inches by ten inches, which he passed over to me. On the outside of the mottled case was the letter *A*, painted in the unusual way that Rafael had always reserved exclusively for me.

The case was sealed. I looked up inquiringly at Paolo. He shrugged affably and said, "Take it back to your grandfather's house, open it there."

I thanked them again and left.

As soon as I got back, I laid the cardboard case on the living-room table and broke the seal.

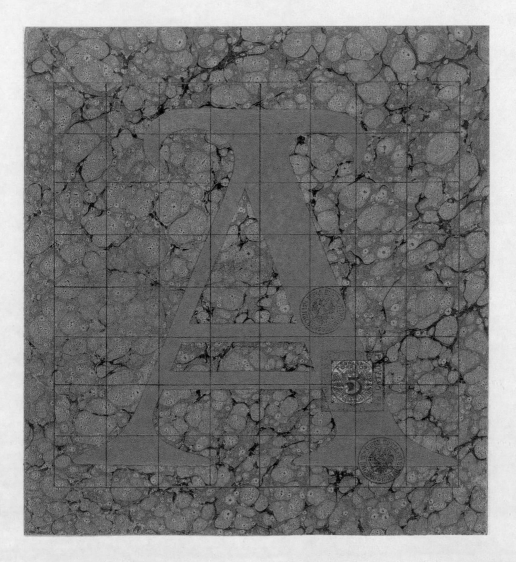

SURREALIST

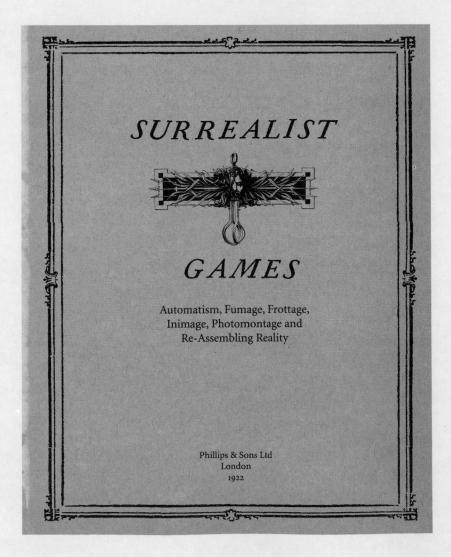

GAMES

Automatism, Fumage, Frottage,
Inimage, Photomontage and
Re-Assembling Reality

Phillips & Sons Ltd
London
1922

Pasted to the inside of the lid was the torn title page from an old book.

I expected the box to contain a letter, maybe some family photos, certainly some form of direct communication, including his last thoughts, advice on life, a reprimand, a declaration of independence, I didn't really know what.

But Rafael was not a regular-model grandfather, and if I'd expected him to turn into one in his latter years, I was much mistaken.

What the box actually contained was a small matted oil painting entitled *Arc of Moons*, signed by Rafael and dated 1937. There was also a kafkaesque, handmade, folded booklet.

INSTRUCTIONS
for the Forgetting Room

❧ Look into the palascope and you will see the verification form.

❧ The button that illuminates the questionnaire also activates the voice control.

❧ Please type in your name.

❧ Nothing will happen unless you type in a name.

❧ Incorrect statements will be erased.

❧ Please tell the truth.

❧ Try again.

❧ If the name you are using has been reassigned, then reclassification can only take place when due process has been completed. Please type in standard code—minus 123456.

❧ Once entered, proceed with the questionnaire until liberation is achieved.

The box and its contents were Rafael's way of challenging me to a game. I knew that for certain.

His work often had a game element. I was familiar with Rafael's fondness for intrigue from my childhood, when he had often constructed treasure hunts and mysteries for me to follow. These conundrums always had a purpose, something he wanted me to learn about.

Rafael's attitude to art was one of serious play. His work was partly surreal, though it never properly fit into that category. It never really fit into any category; he used whatever material or mode took his liking. He may not have received the recognition of other Spaniards like Picasso, Dalí, and Miró, but he had been highly respected by his fellow artists, and if he hadn't been so eclectic, his place in history may well have been more defined.

The first thing that struck me was the title, *The Forgetting Room*. That was the name Rafael used to call his studio in Switzerland. On more than one occasion he'd said, "Remember, Armon, here in the Forgetting Room, the past is present."

I began by trying to see if there was some connection between the *Arc of Moons* painting and the concertina sheet but could find nothing glaringly obvious, so I considered the pieces individually. The painting was of the gorge. Why *three* moons? Something to do with the moons on the front door? I went and looked at the door again—it left me no wiser. The six concertina pages and their questions seemed to hold more hope, albeit of a bewildering nature.

The elements appeared random, though I doubted it—a Rondan landscape with a strange dark figure, a collage of old stamps and maps, a letter addressed to my grandmother, a headless tattooed woman, a wire window along with something that looked vaguely alchemical, and a vast chess game. I stared at the pages, waiting in vain for an insight. At midnight I gave up and put the lid back on the box. However, instead of going to bed as my still-jet-lagged limbs demanded, I made a cup of coffee and went up to the studio.

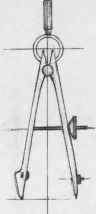

Even without his pictures around I could still feel Rafael's presence. He'd worked right up to the end, I was convinced. I picked up the red bundle again, undid it, and took out a pencil. It rested comfortably in my hand. There was a sketch pad nearby and I started to draw a small compass that was lying on the workbench. For some reason I thought that Rafael's pencil might aid me, but my drawing looked like the usual clinical renderings I'd been obliged to produce back when I was constructing architectural models.

I stood a tube of paint on its end and was having another go at trying to draw more loosely. I started to copy the label, when I heard, as if from a recorder in my brain, Rafael telling me to ignore the surface of an object and to concentrate only on the information that defined the form. "Armon, let the thickness and weight of your pencil mark indicate how sharply the edge turns away. Use the shadow not as decoration but as a means of making the two-dimensional three-dimensional. There is a far greater range between the extremes of light and dark than there is between the white of your paper and the blackest mark you can make. Therefore you have to trick the eye into reading the same range of difference."

As an eleven year old I had only partly comprehended his words, but now, recalling them again, they became direct instruction, and made full sense.

This posthumous lesson left me twitchy and even wider awake. I was still upset that Rafael hadn't left me his paintings; I wanted to remain occupied, so I stayed in the studio to do more drawing. I used one of his old bottles as a model. I thought about Morandi, who'd painted the same jars and cups for sixty years. What must it have been like knowing half a dozen tiny inanimate objects so intimately that you could almost make them breathe?

When I refocused on my drawing, I was quite surprised to find it still rigid but far more solid than my previous efforts.

Even though it was close to three o'clock and I'd definitely had enough for one night, I thought I'd take a last look at Rafael's box.

My subconscious must have been playing detective

while I was concentrating on drawing because as soon as I reexamined the concertina pages I noticed the numbers. *The Forgetting Room* instructions had said, "If the name you are using has been reassigned . . . code—minus 123456." If I eliminated the numbers on each of the six pages, i.e., 1D, 2U, 3E, 4N, 5D, 6E, I was left with the word DUENDE. So I presumed that meant duende was the answer to the first question. I'd heard the word before, but I had no idea what it meant. I nosed around and eventually found an old Oxford dictionary in the living room.

Duende. (doo-) *n*. Evil spirit; inspiration. [Sp].

It seemed an odd combination of terms and then I recalled once hearing somebody on public radio talking about dictionaries, saying that ninety percent of the entries in the Oxford hadn't changed in the last hundred years. This was presumably one of those definitions. It sounded like a Victorian parson's secret cravings for things pagan.

Why had Rafael selected "duende"?

I had no idea.

✺ DAY THREE ✺

❦ I dreamed of an old client of mine—Mrs. Basquers. She was cemented in thick makeup, wearing an alligator stole and a turquoise pillbox hat.

She demanded, "Give up your life of idolatry and become a doctor."

I declined. "I have my geraniums to look after."

Last time I saw Mrs. Basquers for real was about a year ago. She'd come by the workshop to pick up the copy of obscure Finnish verse I'd re-bound for her. As usual her throttled-dove voice irritated the hell out of me. She was cooing over the gold leaf on the spine, which I'd been talked into horribly overdoing, when she suddenly came out with, "And do *you write*, Mr. Hurt?"

Before I could catch myself I responded, "No, Mrs. Basquers, I don't write—I am too aware of the difference between writing for the sake of it and having something to say."

What pompous garbage I speak when I'm defensive.

I'd never tried to write, for the same reason I didn't paint, because I didn't have a clue what to say. To me nothing was ever substantial enough to be worth expressing.

I may have had a craft, but the idea of doing anything more personally expressive seemed irrelevant.

And yet, that past night, there in my grandfather's studio, I'd been drawing for all I was worth. And, for that matter, here I sit, writing these words.

While I was cutting the bread for breakfast, I reconsidered Francesca and Paolo's story about Rafael's paintings. In a way that's exactly the sort of thing Rafael would have done, given away his pictures. I just found it hard to believe that he'd only leave me one tiny oil painting.

I looked again at *The Forgetting Room* pages. I thought about the second question—Nation? After fruitlessly straining to find some obscurely clever clue, I reverted to a more direct approach. The art on that page contained a number of stamps. Rafael used to collect stamps and I vaguely remembered seeing some old spring-back stamp albums in the studio. Sure enough, there were half a dozen on the high shelf. I pulled them down one at a time—printed on the spine of the fifth album was "Germany, Bulgaria, Rumania, and TFR."

Where was TFR?

I flicked through the neat rows of stamps, postal history, and annotations describing dates, watermarks, and printers. Everything was quite predictable and sedate until I got to the TFR pages.

T. F. R.

Having fallen asleep, you awaken in The Forgetting Room.
A flash of something out of focus, then darkness, another
flash and the room comes into view, a couple of blinks,
your vision is clear. You are in an atticlike room, filled
to the brim with dust-bound objects. Everywhere you turn are shelves
stacked with books, maps, postcards, old toys; and cabinets filled
with curios, telescopes, and furniture.

A hard voice breaks the silence. It demands you follow house
rules. It informs you that if you wish to leave this room your only
course of action is to complete the verification form.

The form contains a series of questions linked to objects in
the room.

In order to answer a question you have to discern the information within.

This is an unreliable world you're inhabiting.

You need your pass letter? You find a golden eight-cornered
container. The container is a puzzle, difficult to open, but eventually you find a way in. Inside is a pouch and within that the
letter. You will recognize it.

You are not who you think you are? You already know the tattoo
carrier? Please follow these instructions with great care in order
to rebuild a lost memory.

When a door materializes—you pass into the rest of the house.
Through a window you see a black bull. You hit the glass and it
won't break—the bull snorts. You move on, feeling you will discover
something of worth. But the experience evaporates and you are
brought back from your hallucination into the room. False memories
distract.

§   The Forgetting Room is a locked place. A memory and an exit.

To Rafael his art was far more than a profession, it was the way he conducted his life. His art, his possessions, his philosophy, and his humor were quite inseparable. The studio contained his history, and he wanted me to examine the things there. Was the instruction-questionnaire a guide to help me find something particular?

Question two was apparently answered. The state or nation was: *The Forgetting Room.*

I reread *The Forgetting Room* text. "You need your pass letter?" Obviously a reference to the third question. "You find a golden eight-cornered container." That seemed reasonably straightforward, and I began rummaging around the studio for something that fit that description.

It took me half an hour before I located it behind a case containing a stuffed ibis and a star map. It was a six-inch yellow wooden cube covered with narrow channels and grooves. True to the text it was hard to get into, but eventually I found the trick and it sprang open, revealing a cloth pouch. The pouch was too small to contain a letter; instead it housed a dozen or so old tickets. If one of these was the pass, what was the letter? A second later I found it. One of the tickets was overprinted with a very distinctive letter *A*. My *A*. The one from the front of the case Rafael had left me.

Was I to understand that *I* was the answer to the third question? In what way could *I* be an answer?

The Forgetting Room appeared to contain one other definite pointer. "You already know the tattoo carrier?"

Wrong! I hadn't the vaguest idea who the tattoo carrier was.

I hung around, mulling over everything. Rafael certainly knew how to be annoying.

A shaft of sunlight came through the window and hit me full in the face, jerking me out of my convoluted speculations. I shook my head and resolved to get out into the fresh air. I thought, Maybe if I went exploring a little, I'd come back with an open mind.

Once clear of the house, I found Rafael's game less dominant. I started to take in the surroundings, observing details in passersby as well as in the town itself. In the shopping precinct I watched the families, the swarming children, and the arm-in-arm lovers but saw few unattached people like myself.

When Catherine and I were first a couple, we walked so closely together our hips rubbed. As the months and years passed familiarity created distance—half an inch, an inch, a foot, a chasm.

At night with our bedroom partially lit by the sulfur-blue streetlamp across the road, I would watch her sleeping. Fetally changing from her left side to her right and back again. When she faced me, I felt cornered; when she turned away and her soft breathing no longer beat rhythmically against my face, I felt alone and unwanted.

In Ronda the loneliness still clung to me.

Catherine and I had become friends at our first meet-ing, but it took a while before the relationship progressed. It wasn't that I found her unattractive—quite the opposite, I'd fantasized about her often—but I thought my interest one-sided. Then, one evening, while I was babbling about nothing of consequence, she leaned over and kissed me. I think she only meant to shut me up, but I made certain the kiss didn't stop.

Even toward the end of our marriage there were moments when I'd hold her close, but it wasn't love, it was simply me trying to control the distance between us.

I was still thinking about Catherine when I reached the path that led down to the valley. I wanted to look at the bridge from the base of the gorge. I'd seen postcards in the shops from that angle and I was curious to see what it was like to look up rather than down. When I witness landscape or archi-tecture in a photograph, it often robs me of my ability to see it through my own eyes. It's as if a filter has slipped into place and a flat, standardized image replaces the real thing. I tried squinting and looking at the bridge out of the corner of my eye, then I heard Rafael saying, "If it's too familiar, draw it."

I got out the square green sketchbook I'd appropriated from his studio and tried a drawing. The picture wasn't up to much, but I did manage to rid myself of the prepackaged vision.

After that I ambled around for a while and followed my

nose back into the old town. I crossed the new bridge and noticed that the shadow of the three arches made a colossal face on the side of the gorge. I turned right and then right again, down to the old bridge, then swung around and eventually came out in Socorro square, where I stopped for lunch and considered how best to fill my afternoon.

Ronda's main claim to fame is the Plaza de Toros, the first bullring in Spain to be constructed for classical bullfighting. According to my trusty guidebook, bought for a mere 450 pesetas, it was built in 1784 and holds five thousand people. The book also informed me that the bullring served as the

inspiration for one of Hemingway's novels and that Orson
Welles had spent a good deal of time there.

I'd intended to visit the Toros after I'd eaten, but instead I
found myself scuttling back to Rafael's studio. I wanted to try
putting some watercolor on the bridge drawing. When I did, it
looked a bit sugary—too nice. I couldn't stop there—I taped

the paper to some board and with a wide brush laid a light
monotone wash over the whole thing. A bit better, but what
was I doing? I said, "Grandfather, what do I do now?" And his
words returned to me, "Chaos, order, chaos, order recurring.
Armon, there is a difference between a study and a painting.

Rough up the ground. Then you can begin growing your picture."

I roughed up the ground. I took a bottle of coffee-brown liquid watercolor, thinned it down, and with an old Chinese brush covered the whole surface quickly. Then I dabbed at it with a cloth, to scruff it up further, at first tentatively and then more aggressively. I repeated the process, trying a golden yellow. The result was a mess, though not an unpleasant one. I "humphed" aloud and deserted it to dry by itself.

I'd just had dinner in the Hotel Polo's restaurant and was sitting, chewing nuts, sipping brandy, and thinking about the way Picasso used to sign the tablecloth to pay for his meal. In my peripheral vision I noticed the profile of a very beautiful young woman sitting at a nearby table. Her hair was quite short, coal-black, and her neck was long and naked. For a few seconds I couldn't stop staring; her movements were painfully graceful. When I broke free and looked about, I realized I was far from the only one focused on her. It seemed that half the eyes in the room were pulled in her direction. I kept my gaze on the watchers, men and women compulsively drawn to her. However, something was amiss. There was a strange split in the audience, those on the left side of the room seemed to be responding differently from those on the right. When the young woman turned my way, I understood.

A great scar masked nearly half her face. The disfiguration

etched a ragged shadow diagonally across her forehead, engulfing one eye, the upper part of her nose, and the corner of her mouth.

As a teenager in Chicago, I had had a neighbor whose face had been dismantled in Vietnam and rebuilt in Houston. He had learned to brazen out the stares and make jokes about his own appearance. But this young woman had none of that bravado; she looked calm, like a model wearing a veil. When she smiled, it appeared to be with irony, but I could see that it was her only option—the right side of her mouth was frozen.

My preconceived view of perfection couldn't accommodate her, and while I stared again at the beauty of that face struck by lightning, my tightly held sense of order and composition crumpled in on itself.

⤙ DAY FOUR ⤚

❧ I awoke with a splitting headache and the strange sensation that I'd been in Rafael's house many years before. Of course that was nonsense, but the feeling persisted.

I went out early to try to shake off the headache before finding a place for breakfast. I like eating out, and this is a difficult admission, but I've always been partial to being waited on.

Rafael used to take me out to restaurants. I would sit opposite him and carefully study the menu, my legs swinging below the seat, the upper part of my body very still. He would look at his newspaper. When he felt my eyes on him (he didn't look at the menu; he knew what he wanted), he would lower his paper and say, "What shall we discuss today?"

I never knew what to answer, but it didn't matter because it was just his prelude to saying something like "Don't look now, but that man over there, I think he . . ."

And then Rafael would make up a phantasmogorical story about who the man was, what he did, and how many heads of broccoli he had in his bathroom.

He'd make me laugh so much that everyone would look at me and I'd become embarrassed.

On the way back to the house I passed a bookshop and thought about getting something else to read. I'd given up on the quotes book, it was too turgid, and I wanted to read something about Spain. Instead of buying a book, I decided to look through Rafael's library first.

Once in the house I went to the bookcase in the bedroom and squatted down and scanned the shelves. Nothing really grabbed my attention until I started to get up. Then I noticed the book that had been left on top of the bookcase—*Lives of the Great Spanish Poets*. I opened it at the page flagged by a bookmark.

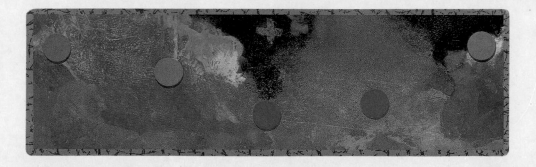

The chapter was headed "Lorca," and there were seven lines underscored in pencil—

The duende is a power.
The duende is of the earth . . . the dark sounds,
a struggle not a concept.
The duende is not in the throat, it surges up
from the soles of the feet.
It is of blood, of ancient culture, of creative action.
It calls one out.

I presumed Rafael had left the book there for me to comprehend the Spanish concept of *duende*. I could see now why inspiration that potent might seem threatening to a stiff-lipped nineteenth-century English lexicographer.

Back in the studio I looked at the previous day's drawing, which I'd virtually obliterated. What was I to do next? I pulled the paper off the card and glued it to a wooden panel so that I'd have a larger area to play with. With a cloth I scrubbed paint into the panel's surface to take away the primed whiteness. After that I picked out little sections of the picture I liked and worked into them, bringing out the light, intensifying the dark. Then I switched to making marks wherever the fancy took me.

Rafael's words barked at me. "That's enough messing about, young man. Either loosen it up or tighten it down, but don't fart around." His voice was so clear, he could almost have been in the room.

I glanced about and spotted the box of old newspapers. I took the first newspaper out and found not more newspapers, but instead all sorts of interesting bits of paper, including torn pages from books, photo clippings, and fragments of aged documents. There were even a couple of letters sent from London to Madeira in 1771. They must have been the things Rafael had collected to make his collages. To my knowledge, most of his paintings had some form of collage element.

It has been said that we think we think then act, but in reality we act then rationalize our actions. I acted, without considering my next move; I just tore up a few of the pages and stuck them on my picture. I worked without making conscious decisions. I glued the fragments in whatever felt like the right place. When I stopped, it seemed to look okay.

As I was putting the remaining scraps back, I caught sight of the side of the box. I recognized the distinctive blue numbers stamped in the corner of the lid; it was from my father's factory.

My father runs a cardboard box company, believes in facts and clear-cut statements, hates abstraction. When I was in my late teens, during one of my occasional attempts to understand my parents' side of things, I wrote to my grandmother asking her what my father had been like as a child. She responded with candor. "He was a pale boy. Born without a great deal of vitality. For a long while we felt ashamed that we'd somehow crushed him with our enthusiasm. But now I don't think so.

"When he was five, he became ill with meningitis. It left no lasting physical damage; however, he had to stay in the hospital for three months while they treated him. We visited him as much as they would allow, but he took it into his head that we'd deserted and betrayed him. When he finally came home, he would recoil from any encouragement and be confirmed in his pessimism by anything resembling criticism. We felt sure his resentment would eventually pass—it never did.

"When he changed his family name from Hurtago to Hurt, Rafael and I thought 'Good, at least he's showing fight and individuality.' But that was his one and only act of rebellion and after that he became even more prosaic.

"Armon, we love him as much as he will let us, though you understand why Rafael and I gave you so much of our affection when you were a child. We had so much left over that your father just wouldn't take from us."

While I wallowed in the light of Marianne's confirmation that my father was a cold fish, I was a little shocked that she would talk of her son that way. This was the first occasion I'd heard anything of their disappointment and it gave me a new perspective. Marianne was growing sick by then and I think she was no longer prepared to keep up pretenses.

My father's negativity pressed down hard on any happiness that came my way. Conversely, Rafael's enthusiasm for life left me feeling inept. I was stuck on the cusp, unable to decide which way to tip.

Moving to Chicago when I was eleven wasn't easy. I spoke fairly good English, but I had a strong French accent and I was teased in school because of it. One particular kid in the grade ahead of me took great delight in cornering me every day so that he could punch me in the arm as hard as he could. Saying, "So, Hurt. Did it hurt, Hurt?" He seemed to find this infinitely entertaining. I dreamed of hitting him back as hard as I could, but I didn't. Nor anyone else for that matter. Looking back, I see I was frightened more by the escalating anarchy of violence than I was by the immediate physical pain. I convinced myself that bullies were something you had to put up with or avoid. By my middle teens

I'd grown tall, and even though I didn't feel any fiercer, I'd developed a half-scowl that seemed to keep would-be harassers away.

I often wonder, Did my father consciously or unconsciously define his pain when he renamed himself? I'd like to ask him, but I know he wouldn't even acknowledge the question.

When I got to university, where I studied languages and architectural rendering, I made sure my accent was dead and buried. As a student I wasn't incompetent—but neither was I a shining star.

Five years later I left Chicago for good and moved to Toronto to make models for a large firm of architects. It was there I met Maggie. She was my immediate superior and by the second day she had me picked out to be her next provider of bodily stimulation. She was a cheerful companion and showed me numerous aspects of sex that hadn't, till then, made it into my physiological vocabulary. But after a year and a half she ended up going to Australia to take on a new job. Maggie's vitality was addictive and the extent of my dependence on her didn't strike home until I was aware of the vacuum she left.

However, her departure led me to examine my position, and after an extended period of dithering, I decided I didn't particularly like my line of work, which had become claustrophobic in its meticulous demands. The previous fall I'd vacationed in New England and felt comfortable there. So for the want of anything better, I went to Massachusetts and apprenticed myself to a bookbinder. My wage was less than meager, but my needs were minimal and I had no struggle with a semispartan lifestyle. Three years later the bookbinder decided to retire and I bought the business with money cashed in from the company shares my father had diligently set aside for me. My father was furious with me, which meant he didn't speak to my mother for two weeks.

My father's reaction was typical of his attitude toward my mother. Having distanced himself from his own parents in the form of an extended sulk, he married my mother to be the vessel into which he could slowly pour his dissatisfaction. My mother's own mother was an inveterate nag and her father a short-tempered recluse who lived mostly in the sanctuary of his garden shed. My mother had chosen my father for his quietness, his good manners, and his orderliness. She didn't realize until it was too late that he wanted someone to blame, not to love, and that no amount of control over his environment could satisfy him. By the time I came along she was already reverting to her father's method of dealing with her mother's incessant complaints. Namely that of withdrawing into abstraction.

Between them my parents offered me only limited nurturing, and it was hardly surprising that as a child I'd gravitated to my open-armed grandparents for my hugs, cuddles, and reassurances.

And so the boxes had bought me the bookbinding business and one of those boxes was sitting, staring at me from the floor of my grandfather's studio. Was there significance or symbolism in the three generations being here together? Damned if I knew.

The studio had begun to feel crowded with memories. I looked at my picture: it needed something fresh that didn't originate in the studio, so I went out to scavenge. Rafael called it "trawling," and it required one to walk the streets with eyes firmly planted in the gutter looking for any scrap of paper that took one's fancy. That could have been how I became such a compulsive collector, although it was probably just a response to my father's overt tidiness and functionalism.

The main roads were regularly swept and provided nothing of worth, but down below the hill, in the ruins of the Arab Baths, I found a couple of items that had that special quality of mysterious-fade that worked well in collages. I returned, attached them to the painting along with some other scraps, and after consideration added some more paint.

This way of working was new to me. I was amazed by how much I knew instinctively from having observed Rafael. The layering of texture, the building from the ground, was

like archaeology in reverse—onionlike skins plumping themselves out, one by one.

About four o'clock I ran out of steam and retired to the living room to put my feet up and have a catnap.

That evening Francesca and Paolo came by to see how I was getting on and I took them out to dinner. I was delighted to be with them and in my enthusiasm I showed them the contents of Rafael's box. They could offer no help with the concertina sheet, but they both knew something of the *Arc of Moons* painting. It turned out to be based on an old Moorish legend about the first bridge over the gorge. Francesca told me the story:

The prince Nasar and his wife, Lindaraxa, had been traveling in the north. When they returned home to Granada, they found their servants wailing and tearing out their hair. It seemed that a djinn had come to the palace disguised as a beggar and had asked a kitchen maid for wine. Not realizing who or what she was dealing with, the servant refused. The djinn became enraged. In his anger he stole away the prince's daughter. The distraught royal couple immediately left in pursuit of the djinn and followed his trail to Ronda. Ronda is the greatest natural fortress in all of Spain and in those days the only bridge lay at the base of the precipice, outside the fortified walls. Once the djinn had barred the gate there was no way into the town. Prince Nasar stood at the summit of the northern side of the gorge and called across the chasm to the djinn, begging him to release the child. At dusk the djinn appeared on the gorge's southern edge. He was holding a rope secured to the princess's neck and he baited the prince, saying that he had heard that Prince Nasar was something of a sorcerer and if the prince could take down the crescent moon from the sky he could build a bridge with it. And then his daughter could cross—otherwise, when the sun rose, the young girl would be thrown into the gorge.

Prince Nasar strove all night to find a way to save his daughter, but he knew the task to be impossible because the moon was too large and too far away. Even so, he used every spell he knew to try to coax the moon to come within his reach. However, in the early hours of the morning the prince admitted defeat and sank to his knees in despair. It was then that his wife came to his side and said, "Husband, I have a way to save our beloved daughter."

The prince said, "If it be true, speak now, for in a few moments the sun's rays will pierce the sky and our child shall perish."

Lindaraxa called to her serving maids, who brought forth three pails of water. The prince looked at her and said, "What use is this, woman? How can these buckets do more than my ancient arts?" But when he followed her gaze, he saw three moons reflected, one in each of the three pails of water.

In an instant the prince understood Lindaraxa's wisdom, and using a simple magic, he scooped the three moons out of the water and cast them into the mouth of the gorge, where they floated down and formed a bridge.

The djinn was furious but, as he had been defeated in a fair battle of wits, could do nothing but send the girl safely back to her parents.

Entertaining as it was, the story disconcerted me. It made me feel like I was failing in my unspoken obligation to save someone or something—though who or what that was annoyingly failed to make itself plain.

I complimented Francesca on her storytelling and asked if she knew of any books of Moorish stories. She replied that Washington Irving had written a book on the Alhambra, though she added that I wouldn't find Lindaraxa and Nasar in it because their tale belonged to Ronda.

We ate and drank a lot that night. I told them more about myself than I'd told anyone for years. I didn't intend to, it just came out as the wine went in. They seemed truly interested and their attention made me feel a lot less like an isolate.

Paolo regaled us with stories of how, as teenagers, he and Rafael had roamed the hills around Ronda. He made them sound like perfect comic book adventures. I didn't know if he was doing it on purpose, but he was bringing my grandfather to life for me.

Francesca spoke of Marianne and Rafael's arrival in Ronda. Rafael and Paolo had been so pleased to see each other that she and Marianne had been left to introduce themselves. Francesca said it could have been awkward if Marianne hadn't been so graciously open. She'd been expecting a cool French poetess and was relieved to find Marianne warm and easygoing. Later, after they'd become good friends, she discovered Marianne's true depths and her majestic gift for words.

We were the last to leave the restaurant and the staff was thankful to see the back of us so that they could lock up. We walked through the streets slowly, stretching the night out, over the new bridge and into the old town. They finally bid me good night and made me promise I'd come to visit them again before I left Ronda.

When I returned to the house, I spent a short while trying to figure out Rafael's game, but I was a bit drunk and I drew a total blank. So I went upstairs to have a quick look at what I'd been working on earlier in the day. Having been left to itself for a few hours, the picture looked very different. The area with the crumpled-up piece of material in the bottom left corner felt wrong, and I picked up a brush to retouch it. Half an hour later I was still tinkering.

⚘ DAY FIVE ⚘

⅏ In the midst of examining my three days' worth of facial growth, I had a thought. I went back into the bedroom, took out the book on Spanish poets, and looked up "duende" in the index. There were two additional references to the one I'd already read.

All over Andalusia the people speak constantly of Duende and identify it accurately and instinctively whenever it appears. This mysterious power which everyone senses and no philosopher explains is, in sum, the spirit of the earth.

   García Lorca

Duende is silent, near-by, a pregnant, and overwhelming power. . . . It is death, life, and fate . . . the consummation of risk and knowledge. Made visible it is huge, potent, patient, but less tolerant than anything the human will can grasp. Duende is a sweet bliss that will infiltrate the bloodstream like toxin.

   Simone

I headed out to breakfast with "the smoky air of curious possibility swirling through my soul." (Not my words, I stole them from one of Marianne's poems.)

By the time I'd finished eating, my mind had turned to objects and subjects—tiles, doors, windows, landscape, Moorish patterns—things the painting needed. I ran back to the house.

I passed a little boy sitting on a doorstep, cuddling and stroking a silver and black cat. The boy made me think fleetingly of the son I didn't have, and I acknowledged him with a cheerful *"Hola."* But he didn't reply or even notice me—he was too busy whispering secretively in the cat's ear.

Once upstairs I stared at the painting and for a moment I thought, I don't know what to do next. Then I thought, So what—what does it matter whether I know what I'm doing or not? Rafael is here, guiding me, encouraging me, cajoling me.

I worked fast, using his methods, playing with the materials to see what would happen. When the picture started to work in some sections, it became more difficult and the changes I made were less radical, though I still wouldn't allow myself to become precious. I kept going all morning, mostly crawling around on the floor (like Grandfather, I found it more comfortable working flat than sitting or standing at an easel), but eventually my knees became stiff and I got up to get a better look at my progress.

While I was stretching, I thought about Rafael's game and how it was really his way of talking to me. I had to try harder at it. Maybe by examining the studio contents in greater detail I might discover something to help me answer another question. I started looking through a big cupboard in the corner of the room. At the back of the top shelf I found an immaculate 1950s super-eight film editor. It was solid and heavy, about twelve inches high, with a tiny gray screen and a fake tortoiseshell handle for turning the spindles. I searched further and located a small circular tin containing a roll of film. Was I meant to find this movie? Was this some part of his game? Maybe there was a hidden clue that led to the film can and I'd missed it. (Later I matched the little icon on the film can with the one on page six of the questionnaire.)

I loaded the film onto the editor and started to turn the handle; it wound sweetly, as if it had been oiled yesterday. I watched the soundless flickering images of a short, surreal, black-and-white movie. The four scenes were obviously linked, but the film felt clipped and jagged, as though frames had been bitten away from the center, depriving it of any real sense of continuity.

It began with a still of the studio I was standing in. Then a shot of a thin man, playing chess with himself. He had a star shaved into his hair. He turned to the camera, held up the index finger of each hand, then placed them on either side of his head.

The second scene was shot at night and the same thin man was waiting by a gate. A car pulled up, the passenger door opened. He got in. The driver turned his head to face the new passenger. The driver was wearing a black bull's mask. Before the thin man could react, someone behind him placed a hood over his head, and the car drove off.

The thin man, disheveled and running for his life, entered a house. He must have assumed that he was safe from pursuit because he stopped from time to time to pick up and examine some of the scattered artifacts (many I recognized from the studio). He was clearly looking for something in particular. He passed through a narrow bedroom, where two monkeys slept curled together in a small bed. He turned into a hallway, then climbed three flights of stairs.

At the top of the house the thin man came to an open window and looked out. There was a long drop. Startled by movement to his left, he twisted to see the man in the bull's mask charging toward him. The thin man opened his mouth and bellowed in what I took to be outrage. This silent sound brought the bull-man to a sudden standstill. The thin man wheeled and leaped through the window.

Unharmed by the multistory jump, the thin man stood on the ground below. Calmly he started to walk away from the house, while behind him its windows went dark. He turned and, presumably in response to the blackout, walked back around the house to the front door and entered it, and as he did so the house came ablaze with light.

I rewound the film, watching it backward. Then through again the right way. I found it unnerving—it was all symbols and signposts, too specific to be dismissed as a dream and too inexact to tell a story.

I was particularly affected by the mask of the bull-man. Rafael had mentioned a black bull in the TFR text. There was probably a link, but I didn't know what to make of it. Spain's hardly short of bulls. However, there was another image of a bull in the back of my mind, but I couldn't get ahold of it.

What else? The sixth question—white move? The chess player with the star in his hair. Were his two up-pointed fingers meant to indicate a bull's horns? I mulled the images over, doodling while I thought.

I hadn't solved questions four or five yet. If this was sequential (and I had a distinct sense it was), I was probably ahead of myself.

I thought of the man in the bull's mask again, the way he'd charged—and then with the most extraordinarily vivid rush, an old memory came flooding back to me. . . .

One evening, when I was about ten, I was in my grandparents' living room with my grandfather and my mother, who was as usual watching TV, when suddenly she looked up and said, "Rafael, why did you leave Spain?"

Grandfather was clearly taken aback by the question and became lost in thought. When, after a few moments, he opened his mouth to respond, he found my mother, who's attention span was extremely short, engrossed in her program again. She would do that from time to time: ask a question, then disappear before an answer could come—as if she needed to prove her existence without having to deal with the consequences of conversation. Seeing that she was no longer with us, Grandfather turned to me and said very softly, "I didn't have a choice, did I, Armon?"

I didn't know what this meant, but, as any child would, I became wide awake when addressed in this adult fashion. Grandfather said, "Armon, let's go for our walk, there's a story I want to tell you."

We put on our coats and went out into the street. We turned to the left and started out on our familiar trek around the block. He began by telling me that when he was twenty he was still living in Ronda in his parents' house. And then he said:

Late one night, after my mother and father had gone to bed, I was drawing in my room when there was a knock at the front door. I went down and stood by the door, not opening it. These were unsettled days, the civil war was in full heat, and it was necessary to be cautious. A hoarse voice said, "Are you there, Rafael? Rafael, they're coming for you."

I flung open the door, expecting to find one of my friends, but instead the doorway was occupied by Manuel Fajaro, a bitter, thin-faced, and violent young man I hadn't seen since my last day of school some four years previously. I'd heard rumors that Manuel had gone to Seville and become a member of one of the Nationalists' death squads.

In his left hand was a piece of red paper. Holding it up to my face, he said, "Hello, Rafael. How are you? Do you recognize this?"

I knew exactly what it was, and I also knew that my life was threatened. But I was powerless to stop what was about to happen. "Yes, Manuel," I said. "It is a Socialist notice. Everyone has seen them."

"True," he replied. "But this one is different. It is more than just a filthy bit of propaganda, it is part of an old game that you may remember."

I shrugged.

"No?" he said. "Let me remind you." And while his left hand was sweeping away the sheet of red paper, his right hand was conjuring from behind his back a matador's sword, which he pointed with an undignified and tasteless flourish at my chest.

"Rafael, we Nationalists felt that today was a good day to be rid of a certain kind of troublemaker. I think you know who I mean—those woolly-headed artists who try to confuse our people by filling their heads with futile dreams. When I saw that the list of prospective candidates for disposal included you, I felt it absolutely essential to come and pay my last respects. I thought I would do you a favor and put you away quickly and painlessly. But then, while I was traveling here, I got to thinking about the time when we were boys in the schoolyard playing 'bullfighting.' And you were the bull and it was my turn with the cape—and how I was meant to kill you, but you ducked under my sword and knocked me to the ground and stood over me and roared and everyone in the playground cheered. Do you remember, Rafael?"

"Yes. It was long ago, but I remember."

"Good, because now we are going to do it again. I am going to take you to the bullring and we are going to play our game once more."

"What if I refuse?"

"Then there is always this. . . ." And he patted the carbine that was slung over his shoulder. "You might as well indulge me, at least that way you'll live a little longer, and you'll even get a chance for a last stroll through our beloved Ronda. Who knows, we might meet someone on the way who'll save you. Though I doubt it—the town seems to be fast asleep."

He raised the blade to my chin. "Come, let us be on our way. Surely you hear the crowd at the Plaza de Toros? They are becoming restless for our entry."

He led me past the House of the Moorish Kings up to the Cassa Arminan, and from there to the Puente Nuevo. As we started over the bridge Manuel paused. "Rafael, I just thought of another game. Let us, for old times' sake, go across the bridge the way we used to, when there were no grown-ups to stop us."

As children, our ultimate test of courage was to walk on top of the bridge's parapet. I had done it a few times and on each occasion the sight of the sheer drop had made my head swirl and reduced my bowels to liquid.

Manuel indicated with a mock-gracious gesture that he wanted me on the parapet. I did as I was instructed and clambered up. The gorge below me was an infinite, indifferent black void. I forced myself to turn away from that vast nothingness and looked down into Manuel's eyes, determined not to expose the fear that was devouring me.

He took my stare as a challenge and leaped adroitly up beside me, careful to keep the sword's point between us. "I will accompany you. Let us step forth across the arc."

We were at the bridge's midpoint when I stopped. If I was going to die, I would at least choose my own time and place. I would rather go here than be slaughtered in the ring. I turned to face him. He could see I'd made my decision. He said with a shrug, "So be it."

I took a few short steps back. Then I put my head down and ran at him. I knew exactly how it would transpire. He would wait until I was almost on him, then he would lean in from the edge, I would try to bring my head up to butt him in the chest, but he would swerve his body farther away and at the last moment he would drive the sword between my neck and shoulder. I would topple out into space and he would hop gracefully down onto the sidewalk.

And that is what should have happened, but his blade never touched me. I was three feet from him when he yelled out. His left foot went from under him; his hip cracked into the parapet. He screamed in pain. I tried to leap to the left, over his flailing feet, but our legs became momentarily entangled. I crashed headfirst down onto the road. My legs must have acted as a lever flipping his upward. For a second he was balanced on the fulcrum of his hipbone and then the weight of his head and shoulders took him out of my sight. From my facedown position I couldn't see him fall. I could only hear the receding howl of his descent, followed by the smallest of muffled thuds. I scrambled to my feet. Looked over the bridge's edge into the gorge, but there was nothing to see, only thick, treacly night.

I ran back to the house. I knew if I stayed in Spain I would be arrested and shot. I awoke my parents and told them what had happened. While my mother packed some of my things in an old leather shoulder bag, my father found what money he could in the house and gave it to me. I bid my parents a hurried farewell and left for Málaga, where a friend of my uncle's, who owned a fishing boat, smuggled me over to Morocco. From there I traveled east by road to Algeria, and in Algiers I boarded a packet boat bound for Marseille. Having safely reached France, I caught a train north to Paris, where I settled as well as I could.

"So, Armon, why do you think Manuel's leg slipped?"

"I don't know, maybe the wall was wet, Grandpa."

"I think not. It hadn't rained for well over a week. No, it couldn't have been that simple. You see, his leg just buckled as if his knee had been struck from behind. Yet that was not possible. He and I were the only ones on the bridge." Then my grandfather laughed and said, "Maybe the spirit in the gorge was looking after me. Who knows?"

I spent the evening in a daze. At some point I went out

and wandered about the town, looking but seeing little, unable to shake the extraordinary intensity of the memory of my grandfather's story.

❧ DAY SIX ☙

🐾 **At first light, I arose** and went to the bridge with a drawing board, a sheet of heavy white paper, and some charcoal. I looked down into the great mouth of the gorge and began drawing. I worked rapidly, scratching, pushing, and rubbing the charcoal, filling the paper with black. In half an hour I'd finished and was on my way back to the house. The compulsion to make the drawing had been irresistible, and once it was done I felt relief. Relief turned into excitement and by the time I reached the house I was positively frantic with energy. I skipped breakfast, just grabbed a few mouthfuls of water from the kitchen tap, and made for the studio. I wasn't sure whether to continue where I'd left off or start a new picture. I looked over to the corner of the studio and noticed an oblong panel of wood that was sticking out at right angles from a small section of crumbling plaster. It gave me an idea—a way to expand the painting's surface. I cut a second wood panel, the same size as the first, and began painting on it. After a while I chopped the new panel in half and worked alternately on the two parts. I determined that if they looked okay I was

going to add the two new sections to the original to make it into a triptych.

Just before midday I went over to the Mondragon Palace and took a few photos of the walls and the floor tiles. In an antiques store around the corner from the palace I bought a handwritten accounts book from the 1880s that had an interesting binding, and an even more interesting little engraving of an owl, with two candles on the front endpapers. I should have bargained for the book, but I'd said yes to the price without thinking.

Sitting on a park bench, facing an ivy-festooned stone wall, I examined my purchase further. There were no more engravings in the body of the book; however, there were a

few loose scraps of paper, scribbled lists, and on two of these I discovered further pictures of candles. Why had these particular engravings been placed there? For a second I thought the book was part of Rafael's game, then I caught myself and was amazed at the way my imagination was running riot. I got up and let the rumbling hunger in my belly drag me off to look for food.

In the restaurant I took my time with the menu, considering all the culinary possibilities, nibbling on bread and black olives. At the bottom of the page was an interesting English mistranslation. *Fillet of dreadcrumbs.* I laughed to cover up the shiver that passed down my spine.

I got my film developed and then took the prints over to a color copying place, where I had a couple blown up so that I could use them as collage material. Photographic paper is too thick, whereas color copy paper glues down flat and is more amenable to paint.

Once home, I began painting the panel wings, attaching collage material and bringing the colors into line with the main center section. Something was nagging at me. I stopped for a second. I'd left the concertina sheet open on the little mahogany table and I went to look at it again. Page four had a "$\frac{1}{2}$" printed in the top left corner. I looked in the cabinet and on the shelves for something missing its other half but couldn't see anything that fit. I went back to the painting. Half? Half of what?

I thought for a split second that someone was behind me and I spun around. I stared at the framed photo on the back wall that showed a youngish Rafael standing in the middle of a plowed field holding what appeared to be a crown tipped on its side. I'd glanced at the photo before but hadn't stopped to think much about it. When I looked closer, I realized it wasn't a crown after all but the left half of a star. I took the picture down and turned it over to see if there was anything written on the back. There wasn't, instead there was another photograph. It showed a beautiful, naked, pregnant woman standing very straight and looking with composed amusement directly into the camera. Her hair was long and black and blowing free in the wind. Her legs were buried to midcalf in the dark earth of a plowed field, while her joined hands supported the underside of her belly. The woman was my grandmother and upon her swollen stomach was clearly tattooed the other half of the star.

In the evening my mood suddenly turned sour. I had begun what turned out to be a wild and somewhat demonic daydream of a drawing. It became more and more elaborate and as I embellished it the elation of the day's work deserted me and I felt alone again. I had great doubts about Rafael and the whole stupid business of painting. Duende was unreal and surrealism, child's play. Even the thought of Rafael and Marianne's love for each other seemed pointless.

I scowled at the drawing, fixed my eye on the candle at the picture center, and went hunting for the origins of my bitterness.

From the shadows I watch Armon as he waits for Catherine to return. She was due back from her sister's shortly after lunch and now it's almost ten o'clock. During the evening Armon has passed through apprehension, floor pacing, and visions of catastrophe. He has become scared and angry.

He doesn't want to lose her—he wants her handy. How is he to get by without her? She provides for him. She looks after his feelings (though of course he won't admit to that).

He doesn't really desire her sexually anymore, but that doesn't stop him from torturing himself, imagining her with other men.

It seems to me he has always been undermined by her clarity and conviction. He thinks that if he bends even slightly into her world he will lose all his bearings. But he is not utterly devoid of insight because he knows that it is perverse to need her when she isn't there.

He tries to envision life without her. He doesn't want to. When she returns, he will make an effort to be a good partner. He will make changes.

At three minutes past ten Catherine arrives home. Does he rush to her? Tell her of his fears and resolutions? No. He waits to see what she will say. Her tale of overheated engines and misplaced keys is undramatic, and almost certainly true.

Armon reveals nothing.

I am exasperated by the depth of his insecurity.

The following morning Catherine tells him she wants a separation. He gapes. He knows this has been long in coming, but he pretends not to understand. He considers pleading, but by the time he's run the words through in his head, they seem too premeditated. So he persists in asking, "Why?" She tries to tell him, but their conversation deteriorates into joint recriminations.

He has managed to convince himself that the blame for

their demise sits at her door. He has enfolded himself back into his insularity.

The Armon I've been observing will never stop blaming Catherine—but I am no longer bound by his decisions and I don't chose to carry his burden or live with his bitterness.

Blaming is futile.

In the early hours of my seventh day in Ronda there was a monumental storm. Tailgating thunderclaps rattled the windows, the lamp-black sky spat like a Gatling gun, and lightning bleached hard-white the room. The massiveness of the drama thrilled me, gave me proportion, showed me my real size in the scale of things. Insignificance has its advantages—free will means nothing to the cosmos.

An idea or an insight doesn't come from a single happening, it requires a meeting to alter a perspective. Often it takes a while for the events to collide, but when they do it is inevitable that a change will follow.

I was walking through the rain-flushed streets, feeling cleansed of yesterday's turmoil, when Lorca's words, "Duende is a power . . . a struggle not a concept," rose inside me and crashed against the liberation I'd felt in the heart of the night's storm, and suddenly I grasped a strange reality. Duende wasn't a mere concept, it was the essence of existence.

It became plain that my grandfather had really known duende, maybe not to the extent that Lorca had, but nevertheless he'd known what it was like to feel the electricity rising within him. Rafael also believed I was capable of touching duende's pulse and had tried to teach me, to ease me toward it.

In the past I'd turned my back on Rafael. I'd been angry with my father, who'd lived such a passive existence, and I'd blamed him for my inability to grasp the moment, but it was me, not my father, who had gone into hiding. My father had been true to himself—he'd made empty boxes. It was me who shied away from self-expression. I could choose to listen to Rafael and let him do what he had always wanted to do—show me a way to belong to the present by reaching into the past.

During the morning my preoccupation with Rafael and duende grew. As I painted I could hear him talking to me. It was more than just memory. He fed my mind's eye with cataclysmic images and I saw duende as a spark rising from the earth's core, bursting out through the global crust into an irradiated sky, a soul without limit, an undefinable expression of nature's unrelenting potency.

As the day continued the atmosphere in Rafael's house seemed to grow thick (in contrast to the air outside, which was clear and fresh from the storm), and my physical movements took on the quality of slow motion. After being in an accelerated spiral for days, it was as though I were meticulously watching myself watching myself.

Around noon, as I was coming out of the living room, my

attention was caught by the play of light on the curtain over the cellar door. I'd given the cellar no consideration since that first day when I'd peeked in on its uninviting emptiness. On impulse I unlocked the door, flicked on the light. The three-watt bulb barely illuminated my descent down the four steps to the stone floor. What was I looking for? Hidden cupboards containing Rafael's pictures? I strained through the dimness, waiting for something to catch my notice—and my foot found a missing flagstone. I reached down and touched the exposed, slightly damp earth. The sensation was remarkably pleasant. I squatted down and dug my fingers into the ground, burying them like roots. I breathed deeply, and after a few moments my mind began emptying of anxiety. It wasn't the first occasion I'd done such a thing, but always before it had been in the open air. With the house protecting me the act became a private meditation.

A picture came to mind. Someone was in Rafael's studio, pulling away at the ceiling's plaster, tearing it from the rafters. Hands made a hole through to the roof, where they pushed and worried until a tile gave way, exposing the darkness above. And through the gap that had been forced a hand reached outward.

I pressed my hands deeper into the soil and grasped tight the hand that reached toward me.

When I stood up I felt satisfyingly calm.

In the studio I beavered away at the two side panels. Little by little they started to feel like they belonged to the big picture.

But something was missing. I kept thinking about light passing through windows. What kind of windows? I picked up a coping saw from the bench and cut a small star from each of the panels.

I added a little more paint, cleaned the panels up, and after a short inspection concluded that I'd gone as far as I could.

Rafael told me that when he looked hard at one of his pictures he could remember everything that occurred while he was painting it—voices in the streets, his emotions and pre-occupations. He believed every artist experienced this, but not all recognized it. If that's true, we are constantly sowing external events into our pictures. Could they be retrieved later? Unlocked by refocusing on the details that captured them?

But in Rafael's case there were no pictures around. Were the events then held within the studio itself? Could it be that the Forgetting Room was really a memory bank?

What had Rafael's questions revealed to me? Of the six question pages, I had some semblance of a solution for four of them. I sat down with a piece of paper and wrote down all the things I may or may not have gleaned. Then I started crossing out the irrelevant bits. Eventually I came up with a list—

1. Name—duende and the spirit of creativity.
2. Nation—the Forgetting Room, the studio, and maybe something to do with being held prisoner.

3. Pass letter—*A*. Me.

4. Tattoo carrier—either Marianne or Marianne's unborn baby, namely my father.

It was turning out like an account of the important elements in Rafael's life. If that were so, what could number five the "union card" be? Rafael didn't belong to a union, I'd been through that every time I looked at the question. It had to be another kind of union. Marriage was a union. The wedding invitation I got from Paolo, was that the union card? It fit—but it didn't, because the card hadn't come from the studio and anyway he couldn't have known Paolo would give it to me.

I considered the swords on the concertina page. The only sword in the studio was the bullfighting sword on the wall. Was it Manuel's? I'd already looked in the tiny cabinet underneath it, but nothing inside resembled a union card. I cast my eyes around the studio again, and in the mirror on the opposite wall I saw the sword's reflection. Underneath the mirrored sword was a pile of battered wooden boxes. One of them contained a compendium of games, things like checkers and dominoes. Toward the bottom of the box was a pack of cards. The card on top was the ace of swords. I picked the deck up and peeled off the ace, beneath it I found two cards meticulously spliced together—the king and the queen.

I had been right for the wrong reason, the union card was a symbol of marriage. The king and queen were my grandparents.

On my first search through the games box I'd seen no chess set, but I double-checked to make certain. In a neat little compartment at the bottom of the box I found not a set but three pieces. A white king, a white pawn, and a black rook with a bull's head carved on top of the turret.

If this was the clue to question six, what was white move?

Of all the little sections of chess games on page six of the concertina sheet, only one showed a white king, a white pawn, and a black rook. In that fragment the white king was trapped on the end file by a black rook. The lone white pawn was in a position to come to the king's aid. The move was obvious—pawn takes rook.

What was Rafael telling me? Was I to take the black bull? How? Where? I didn't understand.

✒ DAY EIGHT ✒

ℑ❧ **Midmorning I went** to say good-bye to Francesca and Paolo. I asked them if they'd mind if I took a photo of the painting that Rafael had given them, the one in the upstairs hall. I said, "Just for my private use—sort of a reminder."

They thought it an admirable idea and insisted on bringing it downstairs "where the lighting is much better."

While I was photographing the picture I realized that the image in the center no longer made me think of Rafael's pigskin pouch—now it looked distinctly more alive and fleshy, like a flying lung or a heart. Far from being melancholy, it seemed cheerful.

The Etes seemed sorry to see me go and tried to convince me to stay longer in Ronda. I said I couldn't because of my ticket. Francesca hugged me, and Paolo took my hand in his giant paw and clapped me on the back, saying he loved being able to see Rafael in me.

As I was turning the corner, it dawned on me that I'd totally forgotten about putting Rafael's house in the hands of a Realtor. What an extraordinary lapse. But I didn't want to deal with it right then, so I told myself I'd see about it later in the day.

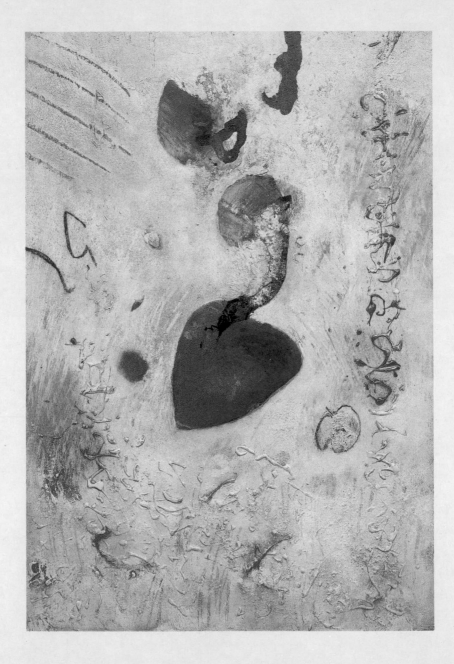

I went back to paint, but then I remembered I'd meant to pick up some postcards, and I knew if I didn't go and get them immediately, then they wouldn't get posted before I left. (Which wouldn't have been the first time I'd ended up delivering people their postcards in person.) So I clattered back downstairs, yanked on the front door, and . . . pulled back in surprise. Standing in the doorway, hand suspended inches from the bellpull, was the beautiful scar-faced young woman I'd seen in the restaurant some five days before.

"Hello, can I help you?" I said. (The suddenness of her appearance had startled me out of Spanish and into my best American.)

She responded in faltering English that accented her French origins. "I'm . . . I'm not sure, is Señor Hurtago at home?"

A multitude of thoughts traveled through my head simultaneously. Was it my grandfather she was looking for or me? What did this amazing-looking woman want with either of us? How was I to unlock my stare from her scar? And, more mundanely, what language should I converse in?

I tried to deal with everything at once. Speaking in French and forcing my eyes to address her whole face, I said, "If it's my grandfather, Rafael, you want, I'm afraid he died a few months back. Can I help?"

She made no attempt to hide her shock. "I'm sorry. Yes. It was your grandfather I came to see. I had no idea he was dead. I came a couple of days ago, but there was nobody home. I've only been back in Ronda for a week."

"Did you know him well?" I asked. Then, before she could reply, I said, "I'm sorry, I'm being inhospitable, please come in."

She hovered for a second before stepping inside. When we were seated in the living room, she said, "To answer your question, yes and no. I saw him only intermittently, but he meant a lot to me." She stopped speaking and tilted her head to one side. I guessed she was determining whether she should say more.

I said, "Please carry on."

She looked at me very directly, weighing me up, then she continued, "My mother was an old friend of your grandmother's and when I was a girl she brought me to visit. I was just recovering from my accident, and my face was still raw. I was desperately shy and didn't want anyone looking at me. Your grandparents were wonderful. Rafael in particular was unbelievably kind. He gave me all his attention, made me laugh, told me that I was always to be proud and show myself. He said that I would never have to worry about shallow-souled suitors and that I had a beauty that would be seen by those with a real eye. He was, of course, saying the things I wanted to hear and I adored him for it. After that, whenever I came to Ronda I visited him. I'm so sorry to hear of his death, but—and I hope you don't mind me saying so—I'm sure he was not disappointed with his life."

It was such an unusually matter-of-fact thing to say, and I liked the sentiment enormously.

I said, "I agree wholeheartedly."

That exchange seemed to signify the beginning of an understanding between us, and we talked comfortably from then on. She was happy to be able to air her memories of Rafael. And I, in turn, found myself speaking about the disappointment I felt with myself at not having come to see my grandfather when my grandmother died.

By then I was seeing the scar as an integral part of her features. I noticed that she asked and answered questions openly, with equal interest. It was very refreshing.

I took a chance and asked her how the accident had happened. She answered with the same forthrightness she'd exhibited on any other subject. Boiling oil from a frying pan had reshaped her appearance. She said she felt lucky her eyes were unharmed. And that Rafael had been right, the more vain members of the male species had avoided her, and for that she was content.

I wondered if she was involved with anyone and I couldn't stop myself from glancing down at her left hand to see if she wore a ring. She didn't, but she saw me looking and grinned slightly.

The first time I'd seen her I'd thought that the unmoving

corner of her mouth must limit her speech, but it didn't at all. Her voice was easy and quite lovely. Our conversation progressed and I was interested in everything she had to say, but I also noticed that I was gradually becoming aware of the lightness of her summer dress and the attractiveness of her body beneath it. I tried very hard not to be self-conscious.

When she finally got up to go, I said, "Are you staying in Ronda for long?"

"For a few months. What about you?"

"I'm leaving tomorrow, but I've been thinking about coming back soon for a longer visit." As I said this, I thought, This is new, when did I decide that?

She smiled her half-smile and said, "Rafael spoke of you as his grandson. I'm afraid I don't know your name."

"Armon," I said. "And yours?"

"Ceres."

I paused, gathering myself. I said, "Maybe I'll see you again when I return to Spain?"

"I would like that very much," she replied.

I walked the hills all afternoon, and for a short while I thought again about Catherine. With the blaming over, I was able to let her go in a way that I'd never found possible before. I let pass the wasted possibilities, too. I accepted that what had happened had been inevitable. I'd been too scared to love her properly. She'd tried to reach out to me, but my defenses had remained unbreached. I knew I would always miss her. And I knew it wouldn't stop me from finding someone new. Next time I would force myself to come out from behind my barricade.

My thoughts moved on, roaming aimlessly over childhood, people I'd liked and disliked, experiences happy and unhappy. It sounds bland but it wasn't; it was a noncritical survey—an observation of the past devoid of judgment—the first step of self-acceptance.

Before leaving the house I'd had the rare foresight to make myself a picnic, and when I grew tired, I sat on a smooth white rock to unpack my meal. I devoured the ham, bread, and dates ravenously. I stayed there propped against the jutting bow of a tree, gazing out at the plain, envisaging a great army of Moorish horsemen swarming across the tundra, a fog of burnt-orange dust pluming around them. I saw patterns within the landscape. On a paper scrap salvaged from my pocket, I traced the lines, and when my eyes became weighty, I lay down and slept in the late-afternoon sun.

I dreamed of Rafael and Marianne. The king and the queen. They were lying where I was lying, yet the landscape was different, the hills and mountains more rounded, softer and ultramarine in hue. Marianne was whispering in Rafael's ear. "*. . . and the Andalusian girls with flowers in their hair . . . and I said, Yes . . . yes.*"

Was she mocking or courting him?

He didn't open his eyes, he played dead, though he'd guessed where her mind was traveling. Awareness of Marianne's desire acted as a mercurial aphrodisiac sliding through his veins, and his hunger for her multiplied with each second he remained still. But he was determined to pay back her teasing, so he waited until she'd risen before he came alive. Snatching her leg, he pulled her back down. She cried out and they wrestled with pretend ferocity, their struggles feeding each other's fervor. Her skirt riding her thighs. Her nipples vermilion in the sunlight. And then with a final surge of determination she rose above him, her head over his, and she was laughing in triumph as she took him far inside her.

The images stayed with me throughout my dusk-mellowed walk back to the town. Far from being voyeuristic, the dream had felt like an invitation, a welcome to participate in events of another magnitude.

It was my last evening in the studio and I was determined to find an end to Rafael's game before I left. I still half clung to the possibility that he hadn't given away all his pictures and that if only I got all the clues worked out they'd lead me to the place where I'd find them. For the umpteenth time I went back to the cardboard case. Looked at, read, and reread everything that was there. I was pretty sure I had all the answers. I just couldn't see what they added up to.

An hour later I asked myself, What if the concertina sheet was not the answer? What if the *Arc of Moons* painting was the real clue? I thought about Francesca's story about Prince Nasar. What if Rafael had primed her to tell it to me, and she and Paolo were a party to the game?

Of course they were! Hadn't they already given me the wedding invitation? Rafael would have needed someone there to jog me along if I got stuck.

I looked at the painting. I thought about the story. What was at its center? The djinn refusing to give the child up. How was the child returned? By the mother's wisdom and the father's persistence. I'd persisted, but what was the wisdom?

I looked at the picture again. The moons formed the arches of the invisible bridge. The invisible bridge. Was there an invisible bridge in the room? I madly looked through the shelves, cupboards, and cabinets. Nothing made me think of a bridge.

Back to the story. The answer had to be in the solution. Where had Lindaraxa found the solution?

In a wooden bucket.

I glanced over at the corner of the room. Rafael's trash bin was a wooden bucket.

I walked slowly over to it. It was empty apart from the paper lining at the bottom.

I pulled out the paper, turned it over, and read.

I have raised three arches and with a clumsy hand have placed in them the muse, the angel and the duende.

Through these empty arches enters a wind of the mind, which blows over the heads of the dead insistently, searching for new landscapes, accents we never knew.

García Lorca

I looked down again at the bucket—a thin layer of soil covered its base. Pushing the tips of my fingers into the earth, I came out with an inch-long Moorish silver moon.

Was that it? No paintings? No Holy Grail or Philosopher's Stone? Had I struggled so hard for a beautiful little trinket? Were the questions just a surrealist's mind game? Had my grandfather been playing with me, teasing me? All that stuff about the Forgetting Room lists and duende—were they a mixture of red herrings and random prods to keep me going? Or was there another reason for the game that I was missing altogether?

Because I found no immediate answer I became angry. I felt toyed with, and I didn't like it.

I almost walked out of the studio and then I said to myself, If that was Rafael's idea of the art of communication, it wasn't mine. And I went back to work on my picture.

I screwed on the panel wings to complete the triptych and fiddled moodily with the hinges. I was being petulant and I knew it. I tugged off a piece of paper and blackened the

exposed area beneath. Using the same brush, I retouched the door handles at the top of the center panel. A few seconds later I saw what I'd done. I'd transformed them into a span of four crescent moons.

It hit me—like a whopping great thunderclap. The realization made me laugh out loud, and its echo set in motion a chain reaction.

The obvious bowed and revealed itself to me—Rafael knew that I didn't need to inherit his paintings—only his desire to paint. He had been distracting me with the game in order to let the Forgetting Room teach me about painting.

But there was still more. I could feel it. Rafael had needed me as much as I needed him. As I acknowledged the implications of our dual reliance, the elements of Rafael's life began to take form inside me. I felt as if I were dissolving into the room. I became aware of some fundamental difference in my perception. I could, I was certain, sense my grandfather's presence. It was as though two eras were coexisting in one space. I saw and heard two sets of sounds and images. Mine and another, more faint, behind it. I couldn't see Rafael, but I knew he was there. I called his name, but my voice hit a wall of cotton wool. My loudness had pushed him aside, then gradually I felt his presence again, muffled, as if farther away. I heard a tapping noise downstairs, followed by a slight draft and sounds that could have been whispered voices. He must have gone downstairs, so I followed. But he wasn't there. I shivered. There was something wrong, and I felt frightened. He had left the house. I opened the door and went out into the bright moonlit night. There was a flicker of shadows passing around the corner. I ran to catch up, but no one was there. I ran for fifty yards, then stopped, panting noisily—I held my breath while I strained for the sound of footfalls. Nothing.

Nothing. Then I heard them coming—two distinct sets of steps. After a moment I saw them, Rafael walking in front and behind him a dark man in black brandishing a matador's sword. With a sudden rush of horror I realized what was before me. The second man could only have been Manuel Fajaro and somehow I was witnessing a replay of the night he tried to kill my grandfather. The figures walked past me down to the bridge. I followed, bewildered and excited by such an inexplicable happening. I heard their exchanges just as Grandfather had related them. I saw them climb onto the parapet. When Rafael charged, I was standing only a couple of feet from Manuel's position on the bridge wall.

I watched with a trancelike fascination as the play was acted out. I knew what was about to occur. The events were preordained—or were they? I had a terrible moment of doubt. What if it happened differently? My grandfather's plight was hopeless, Manuel looked so composed, so balanced. What if Manuel didn't slip? What if he struck Rafael down? If my grandfather died, would I no longer exist? A desperation gripped me. I had to do something. Manuel and Rafael were ghostly images, nothing I could do could possibly affect them. But I was responsible for my fate—so I struck out, I tried to punch Manuel's leg. I made no firm contact, my arm passed cleanly through the vision, and yet I felt the slightest sensation of resistance. Enough, just enough, so it seemed, to disrupt the equilibrium of Manuel's image. His knee gave way under him. He cried out. My grandfather came crashing onto the road while his would-be executioner toppled into the gorge. I stood frozen, eyes shut tight, hardly able to take in what had happened. Had I changed history? No. Instead I had confirmed it. I had sealed my own being. I had tied myself irrevocably to the past and I had committed myself to existence. When I opened my eyes, the vision was gone. My grandfather was no longer at my feet and there was no sound echoing up from the gorge. I looked over the bridge's edge; a bat passed out from under the main arch. I was alone again. I stayed on the bridge, thinking about Rafael and how he had fought for his life. Of his desire to survive, to create. About the rising spark that he believed in.

I realized that I had repeatedly doused the embers striving to ignite within me. Now, I felt their tiny heat.

These weren't thoughts, they were knowings. I had scaled the crescent moon, scrambled over my father's hollow pain, and joined my grandfather, and his father's father and all of the bones beneath us. I was more than me, more than my grandfather, I was each and every one of my ancestors.

I walked back to the house, returning to myself, yet remaining with my grandfather. Elated that our respective prisons had been demolished.

I put my hand in my pocket and touched the silver Moorish moon nestling there. I felt the wind. I wanted to eat the sky, dance a jig, marry the world. I could feel the earth prickling through the soles of my feet.

⊰ DAY NINE ⊱

I walked down the road to the bridge.

At the spot where Manuel fell, I stopped and looked into the gorge.

I spoke silently with Rafael, telling him that I had decided to return my name to Hurtago.

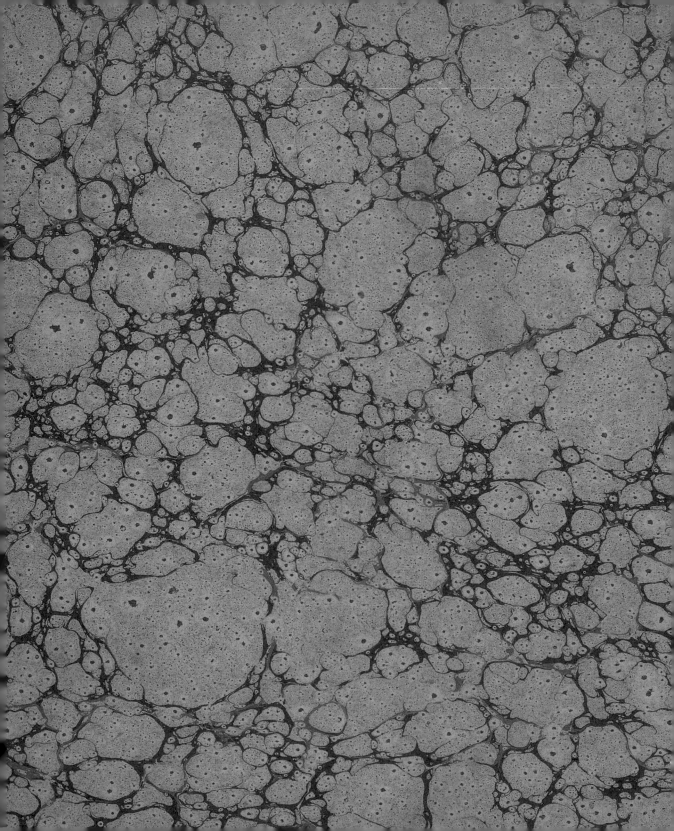